CHRISTMAS MIRACLE FOR TWO

KAYLA LOWE

MORE OF MY BOOKS

<u>Series</u>

<u>Women of the Bible Fiction</u>

<u>Ruth</u>
<u>Esther</u>
<u>Rachel</u>
<u>Hannah</u>
<u>Deborah</u>

<u>Charms of the Chaste Court</u>

A Courtship in Covent Garden
Whispers in Westminster
Romance in Regent's Park
Serenade on Strand Street
Treasure in Tower Bridge

<u>Sweet Honey by the Sea</u>

<u>The Beekeeper's Secret (Book 1)</u>
<u>A Royal Honeycomb (Book 2)</u>
<u>Bees in Blossom (Book 3)</u>

Honeyed Kisses (Book 4)
Blooming Forever (Book 5)

Strawberry Beach Series

Beachside Lessons (Book 1)
Beachside Lessons (Book 2)
Beachside Lessons (Book 3)

Panama City Beach Series

Sun-Kissed Secrets (Book 1)
Sun-Kissed Secrets (Book 2)
Sun-Kissed Secrets (Book 3)

The Tainted Love Saga

Of Love and Deception (Book 1)
Of Love and Family (Book 2)
Of Love and Violence (Book 3)
Of Love and Abuse (Book 4)
Of Love and Crime (Book 5)
Of Love and Addiction (Book 6)
Of Love and Redemption (Book 7)

<u>Standalones</u>

Maiden's Blush

<u>Poetry</u>

1

Matilda stood on a ladder, carefully draping a string of twinkling lights along the top of the front window. The warm glow reflected off the glass, casting a festive shimmer across the cozy interior of her café. She stepped down and surveyed her work, hands on her hips.

"Looking good," she murmured to herself with a small, satisfied nod. The scent of cinnamon and pine filled the air, mingling with the ever-present aroma of freshly brewed coffee.

She moved to the counter and began arranging a display of gingerbread cookies, carefully aligning each one. The little gingerbread people smiled up at her with their icing eyes and gumdrop buttons.

Matilda paused, a wave of melancholy washing over her. Jim had loved her gingerbread cookies. The first Christmas they spent together, he ate a whole batch himself, grinning like a mischievous child caught with his hand in the cookie jar...

The jingle of the bells above the door startled her out of the memory. Her best friend Carol bustled in, cheeks rosy from the cold.

"Matilda, the place looks wonderful!" Carol exclaimed, unwrapping her scarf. "So warm and inviting. You've really outdone yourself this year."

Matilda gave a small shrug, brushing a stray strand of hair from her face. "Just trying to make things feel festive for folks. I know it's been a tough year for many in town, with the factory closing and all."

Carol leaned against the counter, studying Matilda's face. "And how are you doing? Really?" Her voice was gentle, knowing.

Matilda busied herself wiping down the already-clean counter. "Oh, you know me. Staying busy. Focusing on the café." She tried to inject a note of brightness into her voice.

"Matilda..." Carol placed a hand on her arm. "It's okay to miss Jim. Especially this time of year. But he'd want you to find joy again, you know?"

Matilda blinked back the sudden sting of tears. She gave Carol's hand a quick squeeze. "I know. I'm trying. It's just...harder than I thought it would be. Even after three years."

She took a deep breath. "Anyway, what brings you by? Can I fix you a gingerbread latte? I'm trying out a new recipe."

"That sounds divine," Carol said, allowing the subject change. "And actually, I had an idea I wanted to run by you..."

As Carol chattered on about her idea for a holiday event at the café, Matilda let her friend's enthusiasm wash over her. She glanced around at the twinkling lights, the smell of cinnamon and coffee, the plate of cookies. Maybe a bit of Christmas cheer was exactly what she needed. What they all needed.

With a small, tentative smile, she turned her full attention back to Carol, allowing a flicker of excitement to ignite within her. "Tell me more about this holiday event idea..."

Carol's eyes sparkled with excitement as she leaned in conspiratorially. "Picture this: a cozy holiday gathering right here in your café. We could have live music, maybe a gift exchange, and of course, your famous holiday treats. It would be a chance for the community to come together, to support each other during this special time of year."

Matilda's mind began to whir with possibilities, even as a part of her hesitated. "I don't know, Carol. It's been so long since I've hosted anything like that. And the café is so small..."

"That's part of its charm!" Carol insisted. "It's intimate, welcoming. And you've got the best location in town, right in the heart of everything. People would love it, Matilda. And more importantly, I think you would love it."

Matilda absently fiddled with a strand of garland, considering. It would be a lot of work, a lot of planning. But the idea of filling her café with laughter, with warmth, with the spirit of the season...it held an undeniable appeal.

She thought of Jim, of how much he'd loved this time of year. How he'd always been the first to volunteer for community events, to spread cheer wherever he went. Wouldn't he want her to carry on that tradition?

Matilda took a deep breath, feeling a flicker of something long-dormant stirring in her chest. Excitement, maybe. Or hope. "Okay," she said softly, then louder, "Okay. Let's do it. Let's have a holiday gathering."

Carol let out a delighted squeal, pulling Matilda into a tight hug. "You won't regret this," she promised. "We'll make it an event to remember."

As they began to brainstorm ideas, Matilda felt a genuine smile tugging at her lips, the first in what felt like ages. Maybe, just maybe, this was the start of something good. A way to honor Jim's memory while also moving forward. A way to find joy again, even in the midst of grief.

She glanced out the window at the softly falling snow, feeling a newfound sense of possibility. This Christmas, things would be different. She would make sure of it.

2

The bus rumbled to a stop, its brakes hissing in the frosty air. Peter stepped out onto the sidewalk, his breath forming clouds in front of his face. Main Street looked just the same as he remembered, yet entirely different. The old hardware store had been replaced by a trendy boutique, and the movie theater marquee now displayed art house films instead of blockbusters.

But it was the café that caught his eye. Nestled between the bookshop and the post office, it looked warm and inviting, with twinkling lights strung in the windows and a chalkboard sign proclaiming the day's specials. "Matilda's," he murmured, reading the name. It was new, or at least new to him.

He hesitated, glancing up and down the street. Part of him longed to walk the familiar paths, to see if his old house looked the same, to visit the church where he and Sarah had wed. But another part of him recoiled at the thought, knowing the memories would be too painful.

"Coffee," he muttered, decision made. He could grab a quick cup, warm up, and then figure out his next move. Shouldering his bag, he pushed open the café door, a tiny bell announcing his arrival.

The interior was cozy and cheerful, with mismatched furniture and the rich aroma of freshly brewed coffee. Garlands of greenery and twinkling lights adorned the walls, and a small Christmas tree sat in the corner. It looked like something straight out of a Hallmark movie, and for a moment, Peter felt a pang of longing for the simple joys of the season.

He approached the counter, scanning the chalkboard menu. "I'll have a large black coffee, please," he said to the barista, a cheerful-looking young woman with a reindeer pin on her apron.

"Sure thing," she chirped. "Name for the order?"

"Peter." He fumbled for his wallet, feeling out of place and awkward.

As he waited for his drink, he let his gaze wander around the café. It really was charming, in a homey, small-town way. The kind of place where everybody knew everybody, where the locals probably gathered to swap gossip and catch up on the latest news.

Once upon a time, he'd been a part of a community like that. He and Sarah had been regulars at the diner, had attended every town festival and church potluck. But after she passed, it had all felt so hollow, so painful. He'd fled, throwing himself into his work, trying to outrun the grief.

Now, standing in this little café, he felt a sudden wave of exhaustion wash over him. Exhaustion, and a bone-deep loneliness. Maybe coming back had been a mistake. Maybe he wasn't ready to face the ghosts of his past.

"Peter?" The barista called out his name, sliding a steaming mug across the counter.

He stepped forward to claim it, wrapping his cold fingers around the warm ceramic. "Thank you," he murmured, managing a tight smile.

Just as he turned to leave, the kitchen door swung open, revealing a woman carrying a tray of freshly baked cookies. She had soft, dark curls escaping from her bun, and her apron was dusted with flour. But it was her eyes that made Peter pause—wide, green, and achingly familiar.

"Matilda?" The name escaped his lips before he could stop it, a question and a memory all at once.

She froze, nearly dropping the tray. Their eyes met, and for a long moment, they simply stared at each other, the years falling away, the past rushing back.

In that instant, Main Street faded away, and Peter was transported back to high school, to shy glances across the classroom and secret smiles in the hallway. Back to a time when the future seemed bright and anything was possible.

But then Matilda blinked, and the spell was broken. "Peter," she said, her voice soft with surprise and something else he couldn't quite name. "Welcome home."

Peter swallowed, his throat suddenly dry. "I didn't know you were back in town," Matilda said, setting the tray down on the counter. "When did you get in?"

"Just today," he replied, shifting his weight from one foot to the other. "I needed a break from the city, and I thought..." He trailed off, unsure how to explain the sudden, desperate longing he'd felt for the quiet streets of his childhood.

Matilda nodded, understanding in her eyes. "It's good to see you," she said softly. "I'm sorry about Sarah. I heard what happened."

Peter flinched at the mention of his late wife, the pain still raw and fresh. "Thank you," he managed, his voice rough. "It's been...hard."

"I know," Matilda murmured, and there was a depth of empathy in her tone that made him wonder if she, too, had known loss. "If you ever need to talk, I'm here."

He nodded, not trusting himself to speak. The kindness in her offer, the genuine warmth in her eyes, was almost too much to bear.

"Well," Matilda said after a moment, breaking the heavy silence, "can I get you anything else? A cookie, maybe? They're fresh out of the oven."

Peter glanced at the tray, the sweet scent of chocolate and cinnamon wafting up to him. "Sure," he said, surprised to find a small smile tugging at his lips. "That would be nice."

As Matilda handed him a cookie, their fingers

brushed, and a spark of something warm and electric raced up his arm. He looked up, startled, to find her watching him with a curious expression.

"It's good to have you back, Peter," she said softly, her eyes holding his. "Don't be a stranger, okay?"

He nodded, the cookie suddenly feeling very heavy in his hand. "I won't," he promised, and as he turned to leave, he felt a flicker of something he hadn't felt in a long time—hope.

Peter stepped out of the café and into the crisp December air, the warmth of the cookie in his hand a stark contrast to the chill that swept through him. He paused on the sidewalk, his breath fogging in front of him as he looked back at the cheery glow of the café windows. The unexpected meeting with Matilda had stirred something in him, a longing for the sense of community and belonging he had once known.

As he walked down the quiet street, his mind wandered to the past, to the Christmases he had spent with his wife, surrounded by family and friends. The memories were bittersweet, tinged with the ache of her absence. He had thought coming back to his hometown would be a mistake, that it would only deepen the pain he carried. But now, with the taste of cinnamon on his tongue and the echo of Matilda's gentle words in his ears, he wondered if perhaps there was still a place for him here.

Lost in thought, he didn't notice the figure approaching until they were nearly upon him. He looked up, startled, to find himself face to face with his old pastor, a man who had been a pillar of strength for him in the darkest days of his grief.

"Peter," the pastor said, his voice warm with surprise and delight. "I heard you were back in town. It's so good to see you."

Peter found himself at a loss for words, the unexpected encounter throwing him off balance. "I...yes, I just got back," he managed, his voice rough with emotion. "It's good to see you too, Pastor."

The older man studied him for a moment, his eyes filled with understanding. "I know this time of year is hard for you," he said gently. "But remember, you're not alone. We're all here for you, whenever you need us."

Peter nodded, his throat tight. "Thank you," he whispered, the words feeling inadequate to express the gratitude that welled up in him.

The pastor clapped him on the shoulder, his

grip firm and reassuring. "Why don't you come by the church sometime?" he suggested. "We'd love to have you back, even if it's just for a visit."

Peter hesitated, the invitation both tempting and terrifying. But as he looked into the pastor's kind eyes, he felt a flicker of the faith that had once sustained him. "I...I'll think about it," he said, and was surprised to find that he meant it.

The pastor smiled, his eyes crinkling at the corners. "That's all I ask," he said. "And Peter? Remember, no matter how far you've wandered, there's always a path back home."

With those words, he turned and walked away, leaving Peter standing alone on the sidewalk, the cookie still warm in his hand and a glimmer of something like hope in his heart.

3

Matilda stared at the long list of tasks before her, the weight of responsibility settling heavily on her shoulders. The annual Christmas event was a cherished tradition in their small town, and now it fell to her to ensure its success. She sighed, rubbing her temples as the café's bell jingled, signaling a new arrival.

"Matilda, I hope I'm not too late," Peter said, his deep voice tinged with a hint of uncertainty as he approached the counter.

She looked up, surprised to see him. "Peter, no, you're right on time. I'm just trying to wrap my head around all of this." She gestured to the papers scattered before her.

He nodded, his eyes scanning the list. "It's a lot to take on, isn't it? My sister can be quite persuasive when she wants something done."

Carol, Peter's sister, had effectively roped both Matilda and Peter into planning the event together.

Matilda chuckled softly. "That she can. I suppose we're in this together now." She couldn't help but feel a flutter of nerves at the prospect of working closely with Peter. They had known each other for years, but life had created a distance between them.

Peter pulled up a chair, his tall frame seeming out of place in the cozy café. "Where do you want to start? I'm at your disposal."

She appreciated his willingness to jump right in. "Well, I think we should begin by dividing the tasks. You could handle the logistics—the venue, the decorations, the schedule. I can take care of the food and entertainment."

He raised an eyebrow, a hint of a smile tugging at his lips. "You trust me with the decorations? I'm not exactly known for my artistic flair."

Matilda laughed, the sound warm and genuine. "I have faith in you, Peter. Besides, it's not about perfection. It's about bringing the community together."

As they set to work, the awkwardness between them slowly melted away. The bustle of the café faded into the background as they focused on their shared goal. For the first time in a long while, Matilda felt a sense of purpose that extended beyond the walls of her café.

Maybe, just maybe, this Christmas would be different. With Peter by her side, she felt a glimmer of hope that had been absent for far too long.

As the morning wore on, Matilda and Peter found themselves engrossed in the planning process. They bounced ideas off each other, their initial hesitation giving way to a growing sense of camaraderie.

"What about a tree lighting ceremony?" Peter suggested, his eyes sparkling with newfound enthusiasm. "We could have the choir perform and serve hot cocoa and cookies."

Matilda nodded, scribbling notes in her well-worn notebook. "I like that. It would be a perfect way to kick off the festivities."

She paused, a wistful expression crossing her face. "Jim used to love the tree lighting. He would always insist on being the one to flip the switch."

Peter reached out, his hand gently covering hers. "I'm sure he would be proud of what you're doing, Matilda. You're keeping the spirit of the community alive."

She met his gaze, surprised by the depth of understanding she found there. In that moment, she realized that Peter truly knew the weight of her loss.

As they continued to plan, Matilda found herself stealing glances at Peter. She noticed the way his brow furrowed when he was deep in thought, and how his eyes crinkled at the corners when he smiled.

It was strange, she mused, to find comfort in the presence of someone who had once been a stranger. But as the day progressed, Matilda began to see Peter in a new light—not just as a collaborator, but as a friend.

Together, they worked to create a celebration that would bring joy to the town.

They worked until the late afternoon sun cast a warm glow through the café windows and Matilda set down her pen and leaned back in her chair. "I think we've made great progress today, Peter. The tree lighting ceremony is shaping up to be something truly special."

Peter nodded, a small smile tugging at the corners of his mouth. "I have to admit, I was hesitant when my sister first roped me into this. But working with you, Matilda, it's reminded me of what I loved about this town—the sense of community, the way people come together."

Matilda returned his smile, but there was a flicker of sadness in her eyes. "It's not always easy, is it? To keep going, to find joy in the little things, especially when..." She trailed off, her gaze drifting to the framed photograph of her late husband on the café wall.

Peter followed her gaze, understanding dawning on his face. "Especially when you've lost someone you love," he finished softly.

Matilda nodded, her throat tightening with emotion. "Jim was my rock, my partner in everything. When he passed, I felt like I'd lost my anchor. It was my faith that kept me going, that reminded me that even in the darkest times, there is always hope."

Peter was quiet for a moment, his fingers absently tracing the rim of his coffee mug. "I've struggled with that, with faith," he admitted. "After Sarah died, I was angry. I couldn't understand how a loving God could take her from me. I turned away from the church, from everything I'd once believed in."

Matilda reached out, her hand coming to rest on his arm. "Grief can do that, can make us question everything we thought we knew. But Peter, I truly believe that God never leaves us, even when we can't feel His presence. He's there, waiting for us to come back to Him."

Peter met her gaze, and for the first time, Matilda saw a glimmer of something in his eyes—a yearning, a desire to believe again. "I want to have that faith, Matilda. I want to find my way back. But I'm not sure I know how."

She squeezed his arm gently. "One step at a time, Peter. One day at a time. And know that you're not alone. You have a community here, people who care about you, who will walk alongside you."

As the words left her lips, Matilda felt a warmth blossoming in her chest. She realized that in comforting Peter, she had also found solace herself. Perhaps, she thought, this was what healing looked like—two wounded souls, finding strength in each other, in their shared experiences of love and loss.

And as the sun began to set over the town, Matilda and Peter continued to talk, their voices soft and filled with a newfound understanding. In that cozy café, surrounded by the scent of cinnamon and the glow of twinkling lights, they took the first tentative steps towards something neither had expected to find: a second chance at love, at faith, at life.

4

The church bells chimed, their melodic tones drifting through the crisp evening air. Matilda and Peter walked side by side, their footsteps crunching on the freshly fallen snow. The town square was aglow with the warm light of street lamps and the soft shimmer of Christmas decorations.

"I haven't been to a service in years," Peter confessed, his breath forming small clouds in the cold. "Not since..." He trailed off, his eyes growing distant.

Matilda nodded, understanding the unspoken weight of his words. "It's never too late, Peter. The church, the community, they're always here to welcome you back with open arms."

As they approached the church, the sound of carols filled the air, the voices of the congregation rising in joyful harmony. Peter hesitated at the threshold, his hand resting on the heavy wooden door. Matilda placed her hand over his, a gentle reassurance.

"Together," she whispered, her eyes bright with encouragement.

With a deep breath, Peter pushed open the door, and they stepped inside. The church was filled with the soft glow of candlelight, the pews packed with familiar faces. As they made their way to an empty seat, Matilda felt a sense of peace wash over her, the comforting embrace of her faith and the presence of loved ones.

Throughout the service, Peter sat quietly, his eyes fixed on the altar, his brow furrowed in contemplation. Matilda could see the flicker of emotions playing across his face—the longing, the uncertainty, the glimmer of hope. As the pastor spoke of forgiveness, of new beginnings, she saw a single tear roll down Peter's cheek.

When the congregation rose to sing the final hymn, Peter's voice joined the chorus, tentative at first, then growing stronger with each verse. Matilda's heart swelled with joy, knowing that this moment marked a turning point for him, a step towards healing and reconnection.

As the service ended and the churchgoers began to disperse, Peter turned to Matilda, his eyes shining with unshed tears. "Thank you," he whispered, his voice thick with emotion. "Thank you for bringing me here, for helping me find my way back."

Matilda smiled, her own eyes glistening. "You're not alone, Peter. You never were. And I'll be here, every step of the way, as you rediscover your faith and find peace."

Hand in hand, they walked out of the church, the snow falling softly around them. In that moment, Matilda knew that the seeds of healing had been planted, not just for Peter, but for herself as well.

The church bells chimed, their melodic tones carried on the crisp winter air as Matilda and Peter stepped out into the snow-covered churchyard. The service had ended, but the warmth and hope it had instilled lingered in their hearts.

Peter paused, his gaze drawn to the nativity scene beside the church entrance. The figures, so familiar from his childhood, now seemed to hold a deeper meaning. "I'd forgotten how much I missed this," he murmured, his breath forming a misty cloud in the cold. "The peace, the sense of belonging."

Matilda nodded, understanding the sentiment all too well. "It's never too late to find your way back," she said softly, placing a gentle hand on his arm. "I know it's not an easy journey, but you're not alone, Peter."

He turned to her, a grateful smile tugging at his lips. "I don't think I could have taken this first step without you, Matilda. Your strength, your faith...it's inspiring."

A blush crept into Matilda's cheeks at the compliment. "We all need a little help sometimes. That's what friends are for."

Friends. The word hung in the air between them, a promise of support and understanding. Yet, in the depths of their hearts, both Matilda and Peter felt the stirring of something more, a connection that went beyond the boundaries of friendship.

As they walked side by side through the churchyard, their footsteps crunching in the snow, Matilda's mind wandered to the upcoming Christmas event. With Peter's help, the planning had been going smoothly, but there was still so much to do.

"I was thinking," she began, her voice tentative, "would you like to come over to the café tomorrow? We could go over the final details for the event, maybe share a cup of hot cocoa..."

Peter's eyes sparkled at the invitation. "I'd love that, Matilda. It sounds perfect."

As they reached the edge of the churchyard, they paused, reluctant to part ways. The snow continued to fall, blanketing the world in a serene white. In that moment, standing together under the glow of the streetlights, Matilda and Peter felt a flicker of hope, a whisper of possibility.

Their gazes met, and for a heartbeat, the world seemed to still. Then, with a gentle squeeze of her hand, Peter bid Matilda goodnight, a promise of tomorrow hanging sweetly in the air.

As Matilda watched him walk away, she felt a warmth blooming in her chest, a feeling she hadn't experienced in years. The future, once so bleak and lonely, now held a glimmer of light, a chance for healing and perhaps, just perhaps, a second chance at love.

5

The warm glow of the fireplace flickered across Matilda's face as she gazed into the dancing flames. The café was quiet at this late hour, save for the occasional crackle of the burning logs. She pulled her knitted shawl tighter around her shoulders, finding comfort in its familiar embrace.

The bell above the door chimed softly, pulling Matilda from her reverie. She turned to see Peter, his silhouette framed by the frosty night outside. "Peter, what brings you here so late?" she asked with a gentle smile.

"I hope I'm not intruding," he said, stepping inside and shaking off the chill. "I just needed a bit of company tonight."

Matilda gestured towards the armchair beside the fireplace. "You're always welcome here. Come, sit by the fire and warm up."

As Peter settled into the chair, Matilda busied herself preparing two steaming mugs of hot cocoa. She couldn't help but notice the weariness etched on his face, a reflection of the weight he carried within. Setting the mugs on the small table between them, she took her seat, the firelight casting a warm glow on their faces.

"Do you ever wonder," Peter began, his voice low and pensive, "what life would be like if things had turned out differently?"

Matilda nodded, understanding the depth of his question. "I do, more often than I'd like to admit. But I've learned that dwelling on the 'what-ifs' only brings more pain. We have to find a way to embrace the present, even when it's not what we expected."

Peter took a sip of his cocoa, savoring its warmth. "I've been thinking about what you said the other day, about faith. It's been so long since I've allowed myself to believe in something greater."

"Faith has a way of finding us when we need it most," Matilda replied, her eyes softening with empathy. "It's not always easy, but it can provide a sense of peace and purpose, even in the darkest of times."

Peter met her gaze, a flicker of vulnerability in his eyes. "I want to believe that, Matilda. I really do. But after everything I've been through, it's hard to trust in a higher power."

Matilda reached out, placing her hand gently on his arm. "Take it one step at a time, Peter. Start with small moments of gratitude and prayer. Allow yourself to open up to the possibility of faith again. It's a journey, not a destination."

As they sat in companionable silence, the fire crackling before them, Matilda felt a warmth spreading through her heart. In Peter, she recognized a kindred spirit—someone who understood the depths of loss and the struggle to find meaning in the aftermath. She silently prayed that he would find the comfort and guidance he sought, just as she had in her own journey of faith.

6

The next morning, the jingle of the café's bell announced Peter's arrival, a gust of chilly air following him inside. Matilda looked up from the garland she was draping along the counter, a smile spreading across her face. "Good morning, Peter! You're just in time to help with the Christmas decorations."

Peter chuckled, unwrapping his scarf and hanging it on the coat rack. "I had a feeling you might put me to work today." He surveyed the café, taking in the boxes of ornaments and twinkling lights scattered about. "Where do you want me to start, boss?"

Matilda gestured to the tree in the corner, its branches bare and awaiting adornment. "How about you tackle the tree? I've got the lights untangled and ready to go."

As they worked side by side, the café slowly transformed into a winter wonderland. Peter carefully placed ornaments on the tree, his brow furrowed in concentration as he sought to create the perfect balance of color and texture. Matilda hummed along to the soft carols playing in the background, her fingers deftly arranging sprigs of holly and pine on the tables.

"You know," Peter mused, stepping back to admire his handiwork, "I haven't decorated a Christmas tree in years. Not since..." He trailed off, a wistful expression crossing his face.

Matilda paused, sensing the shift in his mood. She walked over to him, placing a gentle hand on his shoulder. "It's the little things that bring back memories, isn't it? The sights, the sounds, the smells of the season."

Peter nodded, his gaze still fixed on the tree. "Sarah loved Christmas. She always went all out with the decorations, turning our house into a veritable North Pole." A small smile tugged at the corners of his mouth. "I used to tease her about going overboard, but secretly, I loved seeing the joy it brought her."

"Those memories are precious, Peter. They're a part of who you are, and they'll always be with you." Matilda's voice was soft, understanding. She knew all too well the bittersweet ache of remembering loved ones lost.

As they continued to decorate, their conversation flowed easily, punctuated by laughter and shared stories. Peter found himself drawn to Matilda's warmth and empathy, her presence a soothing balm to his battered heart. And Matilda, in turn, felt a flutter of something more than friendship stirring within her, a connection that both excited and frightened her in its intensity.

The hours passed swiftly, and as the last ornament was hung, Peter and Matilda stepped back to admire their work. The café had been transformed, a haven of cheer and comfort amidst the cold winter landscape.

The twinkling lights cast a warm glow over Matilda's face as she turned to Peter, her eyes shining with a mix of joy and hesitation. "I can't remember the last time I enjoyed decorating for Christmas this much," she admitted softly, her fingers fiddling with a stray ribbon. "Having you here, sharing stories and laughter, it's made me feel...alive again."

Peter's breath caught in his throat at her words, a surge of emotion welling up within him. He understood the significance of what she was saying, the trust she was placing in him by revealing the vulnerability beneath her usual strength. Slowly, he reached out and took her hand in his, marveling at the perfect fit. "I feel the same way, Matilda. Being here with you, it's like coming home after being lost for so long."

They stood in silence for a moment, their hands intertwined, the air between them charged with unspoken possibilities. Matilda's heart raced as she met Peter's gaze, seeing in his eyes a reflection of her own longing and uncertainty. She knew they were standing on the precipice of something profound, but the fear of opening her heart again held her back.

Peter sensed her hesitation and gave her hand a gentle squeeze. "How about a cup of hot cocoa? My treat."

Matilda smiled at him, grateful for the change of subject. "I'd love that."

7

The old floorboards creaked beneath Peter's feet as he paced the living room of his home, his thoughts consumed by Matilda and the growing connection between them. The warmth of the fireplace did little to soothe the turmoil in his heart. He stopped in front of the mantel, his gaze falling upon a framed photograph of his late wife, a bittersweet reminder of the love he once had.

With a heavy sigh, Peter sank to his knees, his hands clasped tightly in front of him. It had been years since he'd last prayed, the words feeling foreign on his tongue. "Dear God," he whispered, his voice ragged with emotion, "I know I haven't been the most faithful servant, but I come to you now seeking guidance and clarity."

He closed his eyes, allowing the memories of his time with Matilda to wash over him. The way her smile lit up a room, the gentle touch of her hand on his arm, the way she made him feel alive again after years of numbness. "I can't deny what I feel for her, Lord," he confessed, his heart racing. "But I'm afraid. Afraid of letting go of the past, afraid of opening my heart again, afraid of the uncertainty that lies ahead."

Peter's shoulders shook as he poured out his fears and doubts, his words a jumbled mix of prayer and confession. "Please, God, grant me the strength to face my fears, the wisdom to know what path to take, and the peace to accept whatever the future may hold."

As he knelt there, head bowed and eyes closed, a sense of tranquility began to wash over him. It was as if a weight had been lifted from his shoulders, the burden of his grief and loneliness easing with each passing moment. In that quiet space, Peter felt a renewed connection to his faith, a glimmer of hope that had been absent for far too long.

"Thank you, God," he whispered, a small smile

tugging at the corners of his mouth. "For bringing Matilda into my life, for showing me that love and happiness are still possible. I don't know what the future holds, but I trust in your plan for me."

With a deep breath, Peter rose to his feet, his heart lighter than it had been in years. He knew that the path ahead wouldn't be easy, that there would be challenges and obstacles to overcome. But for the first time in a long time, he felt ready to face them head-on, secure in the knowledge that he wasn't alone.

As he turned to leave the room, his gaze fell once more upon the photograph of his late wife. "I'll always love you," he murmured, his fingers brushing the frame. "But it's time for me to start living again. I hope you understand."

With a final nod, Peter stepped out into the night, his heart filled with a newfound sense of purpose and determination. Whatever the future held, he knew that he would face it with Matilda by his side, their love a beacon of hope in a world that had once seemed so dark.

8

The warm glow of the café's Christmas lights reflected in Matilda's eyes as she wiped down the counter, lost in thought. The jingle of the doorbell startled her out of her reverie. She looked up to see Peter entering, a gentle smile on his face.

"Good evening, Matilda," he said, his voice as warm as the steaming mug of hot chocolate she had just prepared for herself.

"Oh, hello Peter," she replied, returning his smile. "What brings you in so late?"

Peter approached the counter, his hands tucked into his coat pockets. "I was just out for an evening stroll and saw the lights on. Thought I'd pop in to say hello."

Matilda's heart fluttered unexpectedly at his presence. She found herself enjoying his company more and more lately, looking forward to the moments they spent together planning the town's Christmas event. Yet a pang of guilt tugged at her, memories of her late husband resurfacing.

"Well, it's nice to see you," she said, pushing down the conflicting emotions. "Can I get you anything? A coffee, perhaps?"

Peter shook his head. "No, thank you. I won't keep you long, I know you're closing up soon." He paused, seeming to search for the right words. "I just wanted to tell you how much I appreciate all your hard work on the Christmas event. It's really coming together nicely."

Matilda felt a warmth spread through her chest at his praise. "Thank you, Peter. That means a lot. It's been a joy working on this with you."

As they chatted for a few more minutes about the upcoming festivities, Matilda couldn't help but notice the way Peter's eyes crinkled at the corners when he smiled, or how his laughter filled the cozy space of the café. When he finally bid her goodnight and headed out into the crisp evening air, Matilda leaned against the counter, her thoughts swirling.

Was she really developing feelings for Peter? The idea both thrilled and terrified her. It had been so long since she had opened her heart to anyone. The memory of her husband still felt so fresh, so raw. Could she really move on? Was it a betrayal to the love they had shared?

Matilda sighed, picking up her mug of hot chocolate and taking a sip, the sweet warmth providing a momentary comfort amidst her inner turmoil. She knew she would need guidance to navigate these unexpected feelings. Perhaps it was time to seek counsel from her pastor and trusted friend. With a resolute nod to herself, Matilda finished her closing duties, the twinkling Christmas lights a gentle reminder of the hope and possibility that lay ahead, if only she could find the courage to embrace it.

9

Matilda took a deep breath as she stepped into the warmly lit office of Pastor Jenkins. The familiar scent of old books and the soft ticking of the grandfather clock in the corner immediately put her at ease. Pastor Jenkins looked up from his desk, his kind eyes crinkling as he smiled at her.

"Matilda, my dear, what brings you here today?" he asked, gesturing for her to take a seat in the cozy armchair opposite him.

She settled into the chair, her hands clasped tightly in her lap. "Pastor, I...I think I'm developing feelings for someone. For Peter Wilkinson."

Pastor Jenkins nodded, his expression one of

understanding. "And you're feeling conflicted about these emotions?"

"Yes," Matilda admitted, her voice trembling slightly. "I feel like I'm betraying my husband's memory. Like I'm not supposed to feel this way about anyone else."

The pastor leaned forward, his voice gentle as he spoke. "Matilda, God's love is endless. It knows no bounds. Your heart, my dear, is big enough to hold the love you had for your husband and the love you may have for another."

Matilda felt tears prickling at the corners of her eyes. "But is it right? Is it what God wants for me?"

"God wants you to be happy, Matilda. He wants you to love and be loved. Your husband, bless his soul, would want that for you too. Moving forward doesn't mean forgetting the past. It means honoring it by embracing the present and the future."

As the pastor's words sank in, Matilda felt a warmth spreading through her chest. A sense of peace, of possibility. Maybe, just maybe, it was okay to open her heart again.

"Thank you, Pastor," she whispered, a small smile tugging at her lips. "I needed to hear that."

Pastor Jenkins reached out, patting her hand. "Have faith, Matilda. Trust in God's plan. And most importantly, trust your heart."

As Matilda left the office, she felt lighter than she had in years. The guilt that had weighed her down seemed to lift, replaced by a tentative hope. Perhaps this was the beginning of a new chapter, one filled with love and healing. And as she stepped out into the crisp autumn air, Matilda knew that whatever lay ahead, she would face it with an open heart and the knowledge that God's love would guide her every step of the way.

Peter sat in his living room, a framed photograph of his late wife cradled in his hands. The memories of their life together, the love they shared, washed over him like a bittersweet tide.

The peace he'd found the night before had already eluded him, replaced by a nagging doubt.

A knock at the door startled him from his reverie.

"Come in," he called, setting the photo aside.

His sister, Carol, stepped into the room, her

eyes soft with understanding. "Hey, Pete. How are you holding up?"

Peter shrugged, a wry smile tugging at his lips. "As well as can be expected, I suppose."

Carol settled onto the couch beside him, her hand resting gently on his arm. "I know it's been tough, being back here. Facing all the memories."

"It's not just the memories," Peter confessed, his voice barely above a whisper. "It's the feelings, too. Feelings I thought I'd never have again."

"Matilda?" Carol asked, her tone gentle.

Peter nodded, his gaze fixed on the floor. "I feel like I'm betraying Sarah's memory. How can I even think about moving on?"

Carol squeezed his arm, her voice firm but kind. "Peter, listen to me. Sarah loved you with all her heart. She would want you to be happy, to find love again. You're not betraying her by opening your heart to someone new."

"But what if I'm not ready?" Peter's voice cracked, the weight of his emotions bearing down on him.

"That's for you and God to decide," Carol said softly. "Trust in His timing, Pete. If it's meant to be, it will happen. Don't let fear hold you back from the miracle of new love."

Peter raised his head, meeting his sister's gaze. In her eyes, he saw the reflection of his own pain, but also the glimmer of hope. "You really think it's possible? To love again?"

Carol smiled, her expression filled with warmth and certainty. "I know it is. God's love is infinite, Peter. And so is the capacity of the human heart. Sarah will always be a part of you, but that doesn't mean there isn't room for someone else, too."

As Peter let his sister's words sink in, he felt a flicker of something deep within his chest. A spark of possibility, of hope. Maybe, just maybe, it was time to trust in God's plan and open his heart to the future.

10

The bell above the café door jingled, drawing Matilda's attention from the coffee maker. Her heart skipped a beat when she saw Peter enter, his expression unreadable. He approached the counter, his steps measured and slow.

"Good morning, Peter," Matilda greeted him, her voice wavering slightly. "The usual?"

Peter nodded, his gaze flickering to the menu board before settling back on her face. "Yes, please."

As Matilda prepared his coffee, an awkward silence stretched between them. The easy rapport they had developed over the past few weeks seemed to have vanished, replaced by a palpable tension.

"How are the Christmas event plans coming along?" Peter asked, his tone polite but distant.

Matilda's hands faltered as she reached for a lid. "Oh, they're...they're coming along." She forced a smile, trying to ignore the tightness in her chest. "I've been meaning to ask for your input on a few things."

Peter's brow furrowed, and he glanced away. "I'm not sure how much help I can be. I've been rather busy lately."

The words stung, and Matilda felt a lump form in her throat. Had she misinterpreted his interest in the event? In her? She set his coffee on the counter, her fingers trembling slightly.

"I understand," she said softly, her gaze downcast. "I don't want to impose."

Peter's expression softened, and he reached out, his fingertips grazing her hand. "Matilda, I'm sorry. I didn't mean..."

But Matilda pulled away, her heart constricting. "It's fine, Peter. Really. I shouldn't have assumed..."

She turned, busying herself with wiping down the already clean countertop. Behind her, she heard Peter sigh, the bell jingling as he left the café.

As the door clicked shut, Matilda's shoulders sagged, and she braced herself against the counter. Tears pricked at the corners of her eyes, and she blinked them back furiously.

Had she been foolish to think that there could be something more between her and Peter? Had she let her own loneliness cloud her judgment?

Matilda's thoughts swirled, and she felt a deep ache in her chest. She had thought that maybe, just maybe, God had brought Peter into her life for a reason. But now, as the distance between them grew, she couldn't help but wonder if she had been mistaken.

With a heavy heart, Matilda turned back to her work, trying to push aside the hurt and confusion. She had been through worse, she reminded herself. She would get through this, too.

Even if it meant facing the future alone.

11

Matilda threw herself into the preparations for the Christmas event, determined to focus on something other than the ache in her heart. She spent long hours in the café's kitchen, baking endless batches of cookies and crafting festive decorations.

But even as she worked, her thoughts drifted to Peter. She replayed their last conversation over and over in her mind, trying to make sense of what had gone wrong.

Had she been too forward? Too eager? Or had she simply misread the situation entirely?

Matilda sighed, dusting flour from her hands. She knew that she needed to talk to Peter, to clear the air between them. But every time she picked up the phone, her courage failed her.

Across town, Peter sat in his office, staring blankly at the paperwork in front of him. He couldn't concentrate, his mind constantly wandering back to Matilda.

He cursed himself for his clumsy words, for the hurt he had seen in her eyes. He had never meant to push her away, but old habits died hard.

Peter ran a hand over his face, feeling the weight of his own loneliness pressing down on him. He had thought that coming back to his hometown would be a fresh start, a chance to heal. But now, he felt more lost than ever.

A knock at the door startled him from his thoughts. "Come in," he called, straightening in his chair.

His sister poked her head into the room, her brow furrowed with concern. "You okay, Pete? You've been holed up in here all day."

Peter forced a smile. "Just busy with work."

Carol studied him for a moment, then stepped

fully into the office, closing the door behind her. "It's about Matilda, isn't it?"

Peter's shoulders sagged, and he let out a long breath. "I think I've made a mess of things, Carol. I don't know what to do."

Carol perched on the edge of his desk, her expression softening. "Talk to her, Pete. Don't let fear keep you from something that could be wonderful."

Peter nodded, knowing that his sister was right. He had to face this, to take a leap of faith.

Even if it meant risking his heart once more.

12

Matilda's hands wrapped around her steaming mug of chamomile tea, seeking warmth and comfort. She sat across from Peter in a cozy nook of her café, the soft glow of string lights casting a gentle ambiance. Peter shifted in his seat, his own mug untouched before him.

"Matilda, I..." Peter began, his voice low and hesitant. "I'm sorry for the misunderstanding earlier. I didn't mean to upset you."

Matilda met his gaze, her eyes glistening with unshed tears. "I know, Peter. I'm sorry too. I overreacted. It's just...this time of year is hard for me. The memories, the loneliness..." She trailed off, her fingers tracing the rim of her mug.

Peter reached out, his hand gently covering hers. "I understand. Believe me, I do. The holidays have been a struggle for me since...since I lost my wife. I've been trying to control everything, to protect myself from the pain. But I realize now that I've been going about it all wrong."

Matilda nodded, a tear escaping down her cheek. "I've been doing the same. Trying to bury myself in work, in running the café. But we can't control everything, can we? We have to trust in God's plan, even when it's hard."

Peter squeezed her hand, a small smile tugging at his lips. "You're right. We've both been fighting against His will, trying to navigate this journey on our own. But we don't have to do it alone."

The sound of church bells resonated through the quiet streets, signaling the start of the Christmas Eve service. Matilda and Peter exchanged a look, a silent understanding passing between them. They rose from their seats, donning their coats and scarves, and stepped out into the crisp winter air.

As they entered the warmly lit church, the scent of pine and candles enveloped them. They found a pew near the back, settling in as the pastor began his sermon.

"On this holy night, let us remember the miracles that God bestows upon us," the pastor spoke, his voice filled with reverence. "And one of the greatest miracles of all is the gift of love. It is a love that heals, a love that comforts, a love that guides us through the darkest of times."

Matilda felt a warmth blossoming in her chest, a sense of peace that she hadn't experienced in years. She glanced at Peter, seeing the same tranquility reflected in his eyes.

As the sermon continued, Matilda and Peter found their hands intertwined, a silent acknowledgment of the bond they shared. In that moment, they both knew that they were exactly where they were meant to be, their hearts open to the miracles that God had in store for them.

The Christmas Eve service concluded with a joyous chorus of "Silent Night," the congregation's voices blending in harmonious reverence. As the final notes faded, Matilda and Peter stood, their hands still clasped together. They exited the church, stepping into the crisp, snow-dusted night.

The town square was aglow with the warm light of old-fashioned lanterns, their flickering flames casting dancing shadows on the cobblestone streets. A grand Christmas tree stood at the center, its branches adorned with shimmering ornaments and twinkling lights. The scent of roasted chestnuts and hot cocoa wafted through the air, mingling with the fresh pine aroma.

Matilda and Peter made their way through the festive crowd, their breath forming small clouds in the chilly air. They found a spot near the tree, where they could take in the full splendor of the scene. Children's laughter rang out as they darted between the legs of the gathered adults, their cheeks rosy from the cold and excitement.

As the town clock struck the hour, the mayor stepped forward, his booming voice filling the square. "Friends, family, and beloved community members, it is my great honor to officially begin our annual tree-lighting ceremony. May the light of this tree symbolize the hope, love, and unity that binds us together, not just during this sacred season, but throughout the year."

With a grand flourish, the mayor flipped a switch, and the Christmas tree burst to life. A collective gasp of wonder rose from the crowd as thousands of lights danced along the branches, casting a mesmerizing glow across the square. The star atop the tree shone brilliantly, a beacon of hope against the dark winter sky.

Matilda leaned into Peter, resting her head on his shoulder. He wrapped an arm around her, drawing her close. In that moment, surrounded by the warmth and love of their community, they felt a sense of belonging that had long eluded them.

As the ceremony continued with carols and well-wishes, Matilda and Peter basked in the joy of the moment. The pain of their pasts seemed to melt away, replaced by the promise of a future filled with hope and love. They exchanged a tender glance, their eyes conveying the depth of their newfound connection.

The night wore on, and the crowd began to disperse, but Matilda and Peter remained, savoring the magic of the evening. Snowflakes began to drift down from the sky, blanketing the world in a soft, white veil. Hand in hand, they walked through the quiet streets, the crunch of snow beneath their feet the only sound.

They found themselves back at Matilda's café, where a single candle burned in the window, a welcoming beacon. Inside, they shed their coats and settled into the cozy warmth, their hearts full and their spirits lifted.

As they sipped on steaming mugs of hot cocoa, Matilda and Peter shared stories of Christmases past. Laughter and moments of quiet reflection intertwined as they reminisced about cherished memories and bittersweet moments.

"I remember the first Christmas after my husband passed," Matilda said softly, her fingers tracing the rim of her mug. "I couldn't bring myself to decorate the café. It felt too painful, too empty without him by my side."

Peter reached out, his hand gently covering hers. "I understand. The first holiday season without my wife was the hardest. I threw myself into work, trying to distract myself from the ache in my heart."

Matilda met his gaze, a sad smile tugging at her lips. "But we survived, didn't we? We found a way to keep going, even when it seemed impossible."

"We did," Peter agreed, his thumb gently caressing the back of her hand. "And now, here we are, finding comfort and hope in each other."

The candle flickered, casting a warm glow over their faces. Matilda's heart swelled with a feeling she hadn't experienced in years—a deep, abiding sense of peace and contentment.

As the night grew late, Peter reluctantly rose to leave. Matilda walked him to the door, their hands still intertwined. They paused beneath the mistletoe that hung above the threshold, a playful twinkle in their eyes.

"Merry Christmas, Matilda," Peter whispered, his voice low and tender.

"Merry Christmas, Peter," she replied, her heart fluttering in her chest.

Slowly, gently, Peter leaned in, his lips brushing against hers in a sweet, lingering kiss. Matilda melted into his embrace, the world around them fading away until all that remained was the warmth of their connection.

When they parted, they rested their foreheads together, savoring the moment. The future stretched out before them, filled with possibilities and the promise of a love that had been forged in the fires of shared grief and renewed hope.

As Peter stepped out into the snowy night, Matilda watched him go, a soft smile playing on her lips. She knew that the path ahead wouldn't always be easy, but with God's guidance and the strength of their bond, they would face whatever challenges lay ahead, together.

Matilda closed the door, the bell above it

jingling merrily. She made her way back to the cozy nook, where the remnants of their hot cocoa sat. Settling into her seat, she picked up her mug and took a sip, the rich, velvety liquid warming her from the inside out.

As she sat there, surrounded by the twinkling lights and the scent of cinnamon and pine, Matilda felt a profound sense of gratitude wash over her. The Christmas season, once a time of sorrow and longing, now held the promise of new beginnings and unexpected blessings.

13

The soft jingle of the café's bell announced Peter's arrival on Christmas morning, prompting Matilda to look up from the counter she was wiping. Their eyes met, and a smile bloomed on her face, mirroring the one that tugged at the corners of Peter's mouth. Outside, the gentle snowfall blanketed the town in a pristine white, adding to the magic of Christmas morning.

"Merry Christmas, Matilda," Peter said, his voice warm and gentle.

"Merry Christmas, Peter," she replied, setting aside her cloth and stepping out from behind the counter.

They moved towards each other, meeting in

the middle of the cozy café. Peter held out a small, carefully wrapped package. "I wanted to give you this," he said, a hint of nervousness in his tone.

Matilda accepted the gift, her fingers brushing against his. "Thank you, Peter. I have something for you, too." She retrieved a similarly sized package from beneath the counter and handed it to him.

As they unwrapped their presents, stolen glances and shy smiles were exchanged. Matilda gasped softly as she revealed a beautiful, hand-knitted scarf in her favorite shades of blue. Peter's eyes widened as he opened a leather-bound journal, his initials embossed on the cover.

"It's perfect," they both whispered in unison, laughter bubbling up at their synchronicity.

Peter took a step closer, his hand gently grasping Matilda's. "Matilda, I..." He paused, taking a deep breath. "I've been wanting to tell you something."

Matilda's heart fluttered in her chest, a mix of anticipation and hope. She nodded encouragingly, her eyes locked on his.

"Coming back, getting to know you, spending time with you... It's brought a light back into my life that I thought I'd lost forever," Peter confessed, his voice thick with emotion. "I've come to realize that my feelings for you have grown deeper than I ever imagined."

Tears welled up in Matilda's eyes, a reflection of the joy and love that swelled within her. "Oh, Peter," she whispered. "I feel the same way. Being with you has brought a sense of peace and happiness that I haven't felt in years."

They drew closer, their hands intertwined, hearts beating as one. Above them, a sprig of mistletoe hung from the café's ceiling, a silent witness to the love blossoming beneath it.

Peter cupped Matilda's face tenderly, his thumb brushing away a stray tear. "May I kiss you?" he asked softly, his eyes searching hers.

Matilda nodded, a radiant smile illuminating her features. "Yes," she breathed.

Their lips met in a gentle, tender kiss, a promise of love and a future filled with hope. As they embraced, the world around them seemed to fade away, leaving only the warmth of their connection and the magic of Christmas surrounding them.

14

Twinkling lights illuminated the cozy café as Matilda stepped back and surveyed her handiwork. The scent of freshly baked sugar cookies wafted through the air, mingling with the rich aroma of hot cocoa. She smiled, satisfied that everything was perfect for the New Year's Eve gathering.

Peter walked up beside her, sliding an arm around her waist. "It looks beautiful, Matilda. You've really outdone yourself."

She leaned into his embrace, savoring his warmth and strength. "I couldn't have done it without you, Peter. This is our party, after all."

Their eyes met, and in that moment, a flood of emotions passed between them—gratitude, joy, and most of all, love. The kind of love that could only come from God, a second chance at happiness neither of them had dared to dream of.

Matilda's heart swelled as she gazed around the café, now filled with the smiling faces of friends and neighbors. Just a few short months ago, she had been content in her solitude, finding solace in the routine of running the café. But now, with Peter by her side, she realized that her heart had been yearning for so much more.

"Penny for your thoughts?" Peter murmured, his breath tickling her ear.

She turned to face him, reaching up to cup his cheek. "I was just thinking about how different my life is now, thanks to you. I never imagined I could feel this way again, after losing Jim."

Peter's eyes softened with understanding. "I know exactly what you mean. After Sarah passed, I thought my heart would be forever closed off. But then I met you, and everything changed."

Matilda smiled, blinking back tears of joy. "God works in mysterious ways, doesn't He?"

"That He does," Peter agreed, leaning in to press a gentle kiss to her forehead. "And I'm so grateful for the miracle of finding you."

As the countdown to midnight began, Matilda

and Peter joined hands, their hearts overflowing with love and anticipation for the future that lay ahead. They had been given a precious gift, a second chance at love and happiness, and they knew they would cherish it for the rest of their days.

As the countdown reached its final seconds, Matilda and Peter made their way to a quiet corner of the café. The joyful voices of their friends and family faded into the background as they knelt together, hands clasped tightly.

"Dear Lord," Matilda began, her voice trembling with emotion, "we come before you tonight with hearts full of gratitude. You have blessed us with the miracle of love, even in this later season of our lives."

Peter squeezed her hand, his own voice joining hers in prayer. "We thank you for the joy and companionship we have found in each other, and for the way our lives have been transformed by your grace."

Around them, the café erupted in cheers as the clock struck midnight, signaling the start of a new year. But for Matilda and Peter, time seemed to stand still as they poured out their hearts in prayer.

"Guide us in the days and years to come," Matilda whispered, her eyes shining with tears. "Help us to walk in faith and love, always trusting in your plan for our lives."

Peter nodded, his own eyes glistening. "And may we never take for granted the precious gift of this second chance. May we cherish each moment and use our lives to bring glory to your name."

As they finished their prayer, Matilda and Peter rose to their feet, their hearts light and filled with peace. They embraced, the warmth of their love enveloping them like a comforting blanket.

"Happy New Year, my darling," Peter murmured, his lips brushing against her ear.

Matilda smiled, her face radiant with joy. "Happy New Year, my love. Here's to a future filled with faith, hope, and endless love."

Hand in hand, they rejoined the celebration, ready to face whatever the future might bring, secure in the knowledge that they would face it together, with God's love guiding their every step.

EPILOGUE

Sunlight streamed through the stained-glass windows of the quaint chapel, casting a kaleidoscope of colors across the aisle. Matilda stood at the altar, radiant in a simple ivory gown that seemed to glow in the soft light. Her eyes shimmered with unshed tears as she gazed at Peter, his hand clasped gently in hers.

The small congregation of close friends and family smiled warmly, their faces reflecting the love that filled the sacred space. As the pastor began to speak, Matilda felt a wave of emotion wash over her. The words washed over her, echoing the journey that had brought her and Peter to this moment.

"Dearly beloved, we are gathered here today to

witness the union of Matilda and Peter in holy matrimony. Their love story is a testament to the power of faith, resilience, and the healing grace of God's love."

Peter squeezed Matilda's hand, his eyes meeting hers with a depth of understanding that needed no words. In that moment, Matilda knew that their love was more than just a Christmas miracle—it was a gift from above, one that would sustain them through all of life's seasons.

As they exchanged vows, their voices trembled with the weight of their commitment. "I, Matilda, take you, Peter, to be my husband. I promise to love you, to cherish you, and to walk beside you all the days of my life."

"I, Peter, take you, Matilda, to be my wife. I vow to honor you, to support you, and to be your partner in all things, through joy and sorrow, in plenty and in want."

Slipping the rings onto each other's fingers, they sealed their promises with a tender kiss. As they turned to face their loved ones, hand in hand, Matilda felt a profound sense of peace settle over her heart.

This was more than just a new beginning—it was a affirmation of the love and faith that had carried them through their darkest days. With Peter by her side and God's grace guiding their path, Matilda knew that they could weather any storm and cherish every blessing that life had in store.

EXCERPT FROM MAIDEN'S BLUSH

Terror filled her as she ran, stumbling across the snowy terrain. Her arms and legs stung from the icy wind whipping across them. She cried out as something sharp struck her. Pushing past the thorny branch, she felt the cut now upon her visage. As the tears trickled down her face, she felt the salty burn of them upon the fresh gash across her right cheek.

A roar sounded behind her, and she turned as the red Lexus skidded to a stop. A new panic seized her as she heard the door slam shut and saw the figure racing toward her. She turned and fled, faster than before, hoping she could make it to the road just ahead.

Hearing the deafening thumps of the steps

getting closer, she hazarded a look back. As she turned, the strap of one petite heel stuck on a low-lying branch, tripping her. She smashed to the frozen ground—hard. Jerking her foot from the shoe, she scrambled up, her hands stinging against the cold snow.

Halfway up, she felt a fierce tug from behind. Harsh hands gripped her waist. "Where do you think you're going?" The dark voice rasped in her ear.

She struggled, desperately trying to break away, but he was far too strong. She screamed, and his arms tightened across her body, one hand covering her mouth. She opened her mouth and sunk her teeth into his flesh as hard as she could. He cried out in pain, cursing, as she broke free.

She had barely gotten five feet away when he recaptured her. She turned, seeing the rage in his eyes.

Then, complete darkness engulfed her as she felt the blow across her face.

Jack Barringer surveyed the sparkling landscape around him through the window of his dark blue

Corvette as he carefully sped along the road toward home . Despite the snowy landscape, the roads had been freshly plowed and were pretty clear.

The sky was sprinkled with stars, and the moon bathed the scenery with a picturesque glow. He turned up his radio. With the ground covered in a glittery white blanket, he could almost believe he really was in a winter wonderland. He rolled down his window for just a moment to feel the rush of the wind, deeply breathing in the cold, clear air. Ah, there was nothing like a Massachusetts winter.

It would be nice to be home for the holidays this year. Christmas was just a month away, and he had it planned to slow things down a bit and relax until the New Year. Business had been great lately. He could certainly afford to take some time off, and, besides, he needed the break.

He was among the best translators on the market, and the clientèle he served knew it. He was bilingual in six languages: Spanish, French, Italian, German, Russian, and Arabic. That's why he could do things on his terms. His father had spared no expense to ensure his son was afforded the very best education. He could still hear his cultured voice saying, "Trust me, son, this will all prove to be useful someday."

And, oh, how right he had been. Thanks to him, he had an extremely well-paying job and was allowed to travel the world at his ease. Just recently, he'd been asked if he'd ever considered giving speeches about how to achieve financial success. That would have better suited his father's expertise.

As the flurries upon his window became thicker, he clicked his windshield wipers on. If only he'd told his father how much he had appreciated everything. He was surprised to feel a sharp stab of pain at that thought. It'd been three years since his father's yacht had sunk, taking with it the only parent he'd ever known. At first, he'd been filled with helpless fury. Why his father who had been nothing but loving and kind to everyone? Why his father whose every intention had been to serve and glorify God?

He'd raged at the Almighty and pummeled him with unanswered questions until he'd finally realized that it was useless to be angry with him. After all, he was the Alpha and Omega, the beginning and the end. He had to know what he was doing. He must have a reason for all things. Jack ran a hand through his dark hair. He'd also learned that it did no good to dwell on the past either.

All memories put aside for now, he turned the next curve in happy spirits once more but then slowed as he spotted something lying on the ground on the left side of the road. He leaned forward and squinted through his window. It looked too large to be an animal—at least a domestic animal like a dog or a cat. He watched as part of the bundle jumped up and took off toward the shiny red Lexus he hadn't even noticed was there.

Warning bells began to go off in his head. What was this? He pushed his foot on the accelerator.

The door of the vehicle ahead slammed before the automobile took off down the road with a squeal.

Something wasn't right here. That man left with too much haste. Jack pulled his vehicle onto the side of the highway and stepped out.

The form upon the ground wiggled a bit as he started toward it. He heard a faint moan that sounded much like that of a woman. Wait a minute, a woman? His brows furrowed and his progress quickened. Alarm filled him as comprehension of what he had just witnessed dawned.

He knelt over the tiny body, oblivious to the wet snow seeping through his suit, and noted the red marks upon her face. Sympathy and anger imbued him. Sympathy for the poor victim. Anger at the heartless villain who would do such a thing. What man could possibly look himself in the mirror and not feel guilt over a crime such as this? How could a man ever physically hurt a woman and not feel shamed at his actions? He'd been raised to be a gentleman. Ingrained in him was the habit to treat all women with respect. He'd been taught early on never to strike a woman, even if angry. And that was one rule he'd always followed.

He squatted down and lightly touched her tiny wrist. She didn't move. She must have lost consciousness. He gently probed her joints. Nothing was broken at least. Although judging by the marks on her face, she would likely have bruises there and elsewhere.

She needed help, so of course he couldn't just leave her there. He put his arms under her and lifted her with ease, surprised at how light she was. Her long, golden hair fell away from her face and brushed his arms. She winced and cried out in pain. Her consciousness was returning. That was definitely a good sign.

Her lids shot open, revealing big blue eyes surrounded by thick lashes that cast shadows over her delicate cheeks. She screamed and struggled, her fists flying, but weakly. He barely blocked a swing to his mouth, capturing both her wrists in one hand, while still holding her with the other. "It's okay," he said soothingly. "I'm not going to hurt you.

I'm going to help you."

When she continued her vain attempt to escape, he turned her head towards him. "You're stuck out in the middle of nowhere. It's snowing, and if you don't find somewhere warm, you'll freeze to death. Trust me," he said gently. "What do you have to lose?" He wasn't sure if she understood what he was saying. She might have been in too much shock. Nevertheless, she stilled, and he carried her to his car on the side of the road.

Katrina's heart pounded in her chest as the stranger secured her in the passenger seat of the Corvette and closed the door. She watched as he passed in front of the car and got in. He was tall—very tall, at least six inches taller than she was and had dark hair and eyes. He carried himself with the ease of someone who was wealthy and sophisticated. She gulped. Just like Bryan. She shook at the mere thought of him.

Bryan was her father's manager. Her father, David Weems, was a successful lawyer, and Bryan worked for him. He was her father's most trusted friend and helped him with many of his cases. She could see them now, heads bent together busily conversing, occasionally laughing and patting each other on the back. She grimaced. Her father thought of Bryan as the son he'd never had. He depended on him. He trusted him—too much.

She shivered violently. She couldn't remember ever being this cold in her life, wearing only her black evening gown and no shoes. She'd lost those in her flight. She wished she'd have had enough sense to grab her fur coat before jumping out of the car, though at the time her only thought had been to flee.

As if sensing her thoughts and sympathizing, the engine roared to life, and heat hit her face. The stranger in the driver's seat removed his coat and then reached across the car toward her. She recoiled back, eyes wide, scooting as close to the passenger-side door as she could get, prepared to jump from this car too if need be.

The man, apparently, seeing her fear, simply placed his coat on the middle console. "To warm you faster," he nodded toward the coat gently.

"Thank you," she barely managed with a lump in her throat. She took the coat and hugged it around her shoulders as the car began to move onto the road. Suddenly, a new thought struck her. Who was this man and where was he taking her? Panic seized her. What if he were just like Bryan? He'd said he would help, but so had Bryan. What if she had escaped Bryan only to end up with someone worse?

Her hands gripped the edges of her seat tightly. "Where are you taking me?" she asked, her voice shaky.

He glanced at her. "To the hospital," he answered. "I checked your joints. Nothing's broken, but you should still be checked out by professionals."

"No!" she croaked out. He momentarily took his eyes off the road to glance over at her again. "I can't go to the hospital," she fairly shook. Bryan was smart and resourceful. If she checked into a hospital, he would surely find her.

The stranger pulled the car onto the side of the road, and she stared at his huge hands as he shifted the gear in the middle of the car into park. She stared at him warily as his muscular frame turned toward her. "What's your name?" he asked.

She paused. How did she know she could trust this man? Frantic questions ran through her mind, and she licked her lips nervously, her eyes darting out the window frantically. They were in the middle of nowhere. There was nowhere for her to run. Of course, there hadn't really been anywhere for her to run when she'd jumped out of Bryan's car either. She'd just acted on instinct then.

She glanced back at the driver. He was her only means of getting help right now. He was right. If he hadn't shown up, she would have probably become even more lost than she already was and frozen to death. Looks like it was either take a chance and trust him or become a frozen statuette. She would have to trust him.

Besides, if he had intentions of hurting her, he would have acted on them already, wouldn't he?

"Katrina," she answered hesitantly, pressing closer into the seat.

He noticed the defensive gesture, and his voice softened. "I'm Jack Barringer. And I'm not going to harm you. I'm just going to take you to a hospital where you'll be properly cared for."

"I'm not going to a hospital," she stated defiantly with a hint of panic to her voice. He raised his brows and studied her. "I'm not," she repeated firmly, uncomfortable under his scrutiny but adamant in her reiteration.

He didn't question her, just started the engine. "Where are you staying? With family, at a hotel?" His steady gaze rested on her.

Her stomach plunged as the gravity of her situation fully hit her. Here she was in the middle of nowhere sitting in a car with a complete stranger and nowhere to go. No purse, no credit cards, no identification—nothing. She almost laughed at the absurdity of it all. She didn't even have any shoes. Who would have ever thought that she, Katrina Weems, the Harvard graduate, would ever have been so stupid as to screw up this bad?

Her face paled as she thought of how angry Bryan was sure to be. She could only imagine what his wrath would be like if he found her. He was probably right now rummaging through her purse. He would know even more about her than he already assuredly did. He now had her social security number, her resumes and job applications, her money, and not to mention what else. She shuddered to think of him delving in her suitcase.

Oh, why had she been so naïve as to believe that he was only doing her father a favor by coming to pick her up at the airport? Why couldn't her father have just dropped his meeting and come to get her himself? Why did she agree to take an interview in Boston instead of flying straight home to Tennessee from California? The questions kept reverberating throughout her brain when she was jerked back to the present.

"Huh?" she asked, startled.

"I was asking if you had anywhere to stay," he repeated.

She shifted uncomfortably. "Um, no, not exactly."

He flicked his turn signal on and glanced at her curiously. "No problem then. We'll just find you a hotel to spend the night in, and we'll sort through everything tomorrow."

"It's not that easy," she said nervously.

"Why not?" He frowned.

"I don't have anyone, and all of my belongings

—my purse, everything—are gone...with him," she explained uneasily.

He looked over at her and for the first time realized that she carried nothing but the clothes on her back. He let out a sigh of frustration. Yes, he pitied her situation, but he was definitely not feeling up to being this caliber of a rescuer. Having a big heart, he did try to help people in need. The world could be a cruel place, especially to women. This poor girl was proof of that. He felt his indignation rise again at the injustice of what he'd glimpsed. But he'd had small gestures in mind. He'd hoped to take her home to safety and be on his merry way.

So much for a relaxing vacation. Here he was stuck with a young woman who had nothing with her and was now totally dependent on him. *Why now, Lord?* Almost immediately, he realized what a jerk he was being and was chastised by his Heavenly Father. How selfish could he be? This wasn't her fault. He certainly couldn't leave her high and dry and scared as she was. God had obviously placed him there at that moment to help her, and he knew that's what he would have to do.

How was he going to do anything to help someone who didn't even have any proof of who she was, though?

She put her head in her hands, that long, golden hair falling on either side. She looked miserable, her fancy dress torn and dirty. He guessed she was a very attractive woman when not so unkempt as she was now. It was easy to imagine that a man would notice her. But what exactly had happened to put her in the state she was in now?

Compassion and remorse filled him at his selfishness. She had refused to go to the hospital. Was she afraid of being found by her attacker? What exactly had occurred by the time he arrived on the scene? She had nowhere to go. No friends or family in the area, no hotel reservation. Had she been staying with this man? Or was it something else? He hadn't pressed her for answers. She'd been through a trying ordeal.

No, she didn't want to be in this predicament any more than he did. It was worse on her part. She was the one who had been assaulted and left out in the cold with nothing.

"Hey," he steadied the wheel with one hand and reached out to touch her shoulder with the other. Mistake. She jumped at the contact, and he winced, mumbling an apology. She physically gathered herself together and raised her head, looking like a lost little girl. It went straight to his heart. "It's going to be okay. I'll pay for each of us a room. We'll sort through everything in the morning." He smiled. "I had planned to stay a night in Boston before returning home anyway."

She looked at him with skepticism and apprehension before slowly nodding her head. "Thank you," she weakly managed before looking back down as if she were ashamed.

Get Maiden's Blush now!

ABOUT THE AUTHOR

Award-winning author Kayla Lowe writes women's fiction that explores complex themes with sensitivity and depth. Kayla's books delve into the intricacies of relationships, self-discovery, and resilience. From cozy love stories interspersed with a bit of faith to heartwarming tales of friend-ship and suspenseful novels of empowerment and heartbreak, her books illustrate the struggles specific to women.

When she's not churning out her next novel, you can find her with her feet in the sand and a book in her hand or curled up on the couch with her dogs.

Visit her website at www.authorkay lalowe.com.

ALSO BY KAYLA LOWE

Sweet Honey by the Sea

The Beekeeper's Secret (Book 1)
A Royal Honeycomb (Book 2)
Bees in Blossom (Book 3)
Honeyed Kisses (Book 4)
Blooming Forever (Book 5)

Strawberry Beach Series

Beachside Lessons (Book 1)
Beachside Lessons (Book 2)
Beachside Lessons (Book 3)

Panama City Beach Series

Sun-Kissed Secrets (Book 1)
Sun-Kissed Secrets (Book 2)
Sun-Kissed Secrets (Book 3)

❄

The Tainted Love Saga

Of Love and Deception (Book 1)

Of Love and Family (Book 2)

Of Love and Violence (Book 3)

Of Love and Abuse(Book 4)

Of Love and Crime (Book 5)

Of Love and Addiction (Book 6)

Of Love and Redemption (Book 7)

<u>Standalones</u>

Maiden's Blush

<u>Poetry</u>

Phantom Poetry

Lost and Found

9 798822 764976